P9-BAU-091
Would you rather be a Bullfrog?
By Dr. Seuss*
*writing as
Theo. LeSieg
Illustrated by Roy McKie
A Bright and Early Book
From BEGINNER BOOKS®
A Division of Random House, Inc.

Tell me!

Would you rather be
a Dog . . . or be a Cat?

It's time for you
to think about
important things like that.

Would you
rather be
a Bullfrog . . .

. . . or be
a Butterfly?

Which one
would you rather be?
Come on, now.
Tell me why.

Tell me.
Would you rather be
a Minnow
or a Whale?

And tell me,
would you
rather be
a Hammer
or a Nail?

Would you
rather have
a Feather . . .

or a Bushy Tail behind?

Which would feel
the best on you?
Come on!
Make up your mind.

And . . .
would you rather be
a Cactus . . .

or a Toadstool . . .

or a Rose?

AND . . .
which would look
the best on you . . .

. . . the Long
or
Shortish Nose?

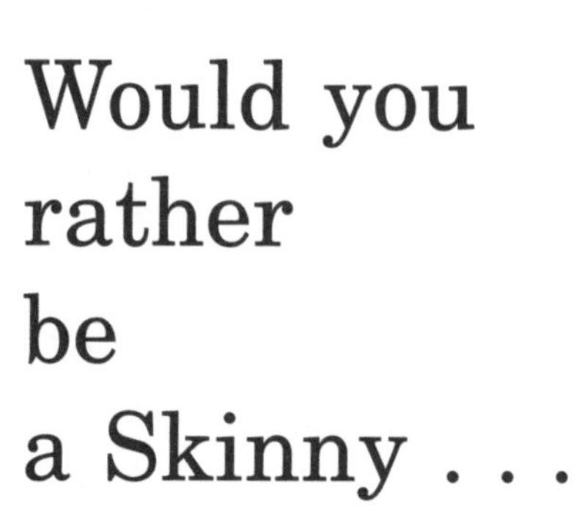

Would you
rather
be
a Skinny . . .

OR
would you rather be
a FAT?

Would you rather
be a Ball . . .

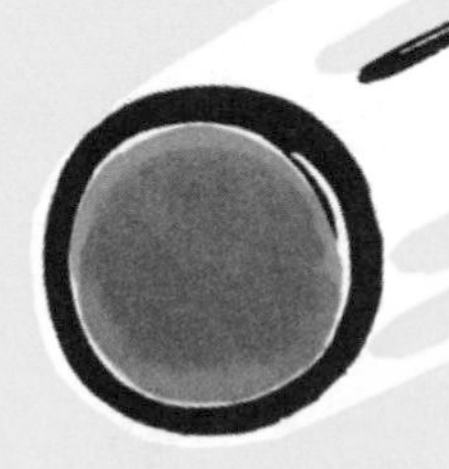

. . . or
would you
rather be
a Bat?

And once more
I'm going to ask you . . .
how about
that Dog and Cat?

THINK, now!
Would you rather be

. . . a Rooster

. . . or a Hen?

(How would you like to
lay an egg
every now and then?)

Would you
rather have
big Moose Horns . . .

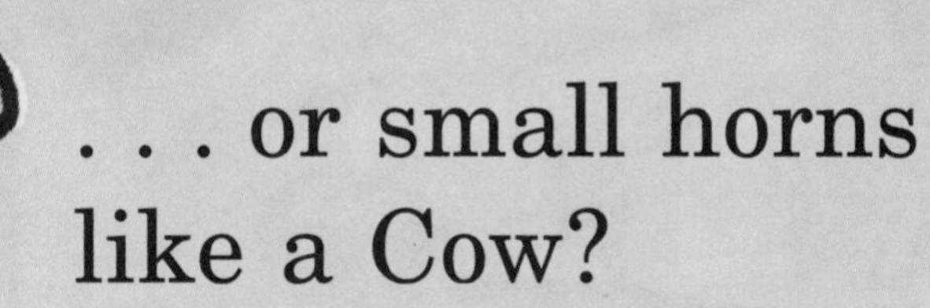

. . . or small horns
like a Cow?

This is so, so, so important
and I want
to know right now!

Would you
rather be
a Bloogle Bird
and fly around
and sing . . .

. . . or would you
rather be
a Bumble Bee
and fly around
and sting?

And tell me,
would you rather be
a Table . . . or a Chair?

And NOW tell me,
would you rather have
Green . . . or Purple Hair?

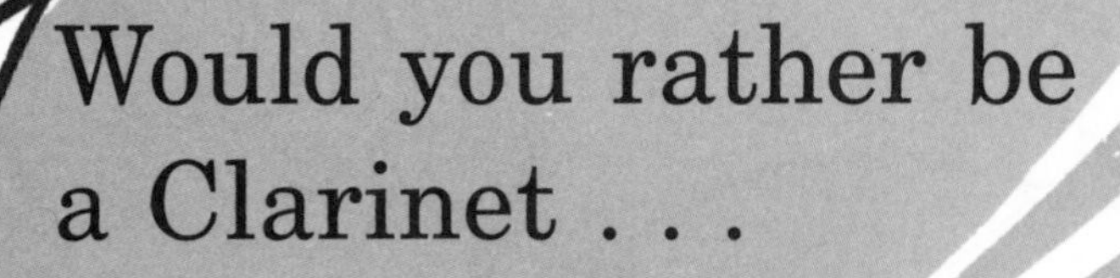

Would you rather be
a Clarinet . . .

. . . a Trombone

. . . or a Drum?

(How would you
like to have someone
going BOOM-BOOM
on your Tum?)

Suppose you had to be
a LETTER!
Well, then,
which one would you be?
Would you rather be a Curly one . . .

. . . like

. . . or

. . . or

Or would you rather
be a Sharpie . . .

. . . like K

. . . or Z

. . . or V

Now tell me . . .
. . . would you rather be
a Window . . . or . . . a Door?

And would you
have more fun

if you had Six Feet . . .

or a Hundred and Sixty-four?

These are
real important questions.
Come on!
Tell me! Tell me please!

Would you
rather be
a Soda?

OR . . .

A piece
of smelly
Cheese?

Would you rather
live in Igloos . . . or . . .
would you
rather live in Tents?

AND . . .

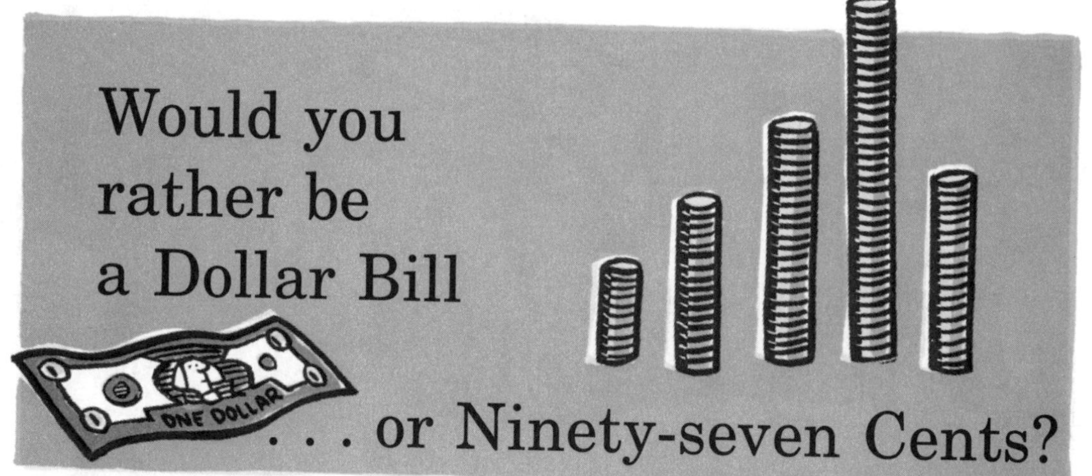

Would you
rather be
a Dollar Bill

. . . or Ninety-seven Cents?

AND would you rather be
a Mermaid
with a tail instead of feet . . . ?

OR . . .

Would you rather be
a Spook
and run around
dressed in a sheet?

Would you
rather be
a Jellyfish . . .

. . . a Sawfish . . .

. . . or Sardine?

AND
would
you
rather be
THIS Thing . . . or THAT . . .

or
the
Thing
that's
in between?

It's hard to make your mind up
about important things like that.

(I can't even make
MY mind up
about that
Dog and Cat.)

Theo. LeSieg

. . . and Dr. Seuss led almost mystically parallel lives. Born at the same time in Springfield, Massachusetts, they attended Dartmouth, Oxford, and the Sorbonne together, and, in the army, served overseas in the same division. When Mr. LeSieg, inevitably, decided to write a children's book, he was, happily, able to prevail on his old friend Dr. Seuss to help him find a publisher. Since then his stories have delighted millions of children around the world.

. . . lives in New Jersey, where (when he can't go skating) he draws pictures . . . and (when he has nothing to draw) he goes skating. The rest of the time he travels—there are very few places he hasn't been. Luckily for us he draws very quickly, so between traveling and skating he has been able to illustrate several favorite Bright and Early and Beginner Books (among them *Ten Apples Up on Top!, In a People House, The Pop-Up Mice of Mr. Brice,* and *My Book About Me*).